A Very Fuddles Christmas

I want to thank my parents, Toine and Dorothy Vischer,
for letting me follow my dreams

• • •

Many thanks to the Karens at Aladdin:
Karen Nagel, Karina Granda, and Karin Paprocki

ALADDIN

An imprint of Simon & Schuster Children's Publishing Division • 1230 Avenue of the Americas, New York, NY 10020

First Aladdin hardcover edition October 2013

Text and illustrations copyright © 2013 by Frans Vischer

ALADDIN is a trademark of Simon & Schuster, Inc., and related logo is a registered trademark of Simon & Schuster, Inc.

For information about special discounts for bulk purchases, please contact Simon & Schuster Special Sales

at 1-866-506-1949 or business@simonandschuster.com.

The Simon & Schuster Speakers Bureau can bring authors to your live event. For more information or to book an event

contact the Simon & Schuster Speakers Bureau at 1-866-248-3049 or visit our website at www.simonspeakers.com.

Designed by Karina Granda

The text of this book was set in Wade Sans Light.

The illustrations for this book were rendered digitally.

Manufactured in China 0713 SCP

2 4 6 8 10 9 7 5 3 1

This book has been cataloged with the Library of Congress

ISBN 978-1-4169-9156-4

ISBN 978-1-4424-3511-7 (eBook)

A Very Fuddles Christmas

WRITTEN AND ILLUSTRATED BY Frans Vischer

Aladdin

NEW YORK   LONDON   TORONTO   SYDNEY   NEW DELHI

Fuddles was a fat, pampered cat.

His family spoiled him endlessly.

One day, a yummy aroma
awakened Fuddles from his catnap.
What's that? he wondered.

He followed his nose into the dining room.

Me-wow!
Look at the delicious meal
his family made—just for him!

Fuddles was about to dig in, when . . .

"No, Fuddles! That's not for you!"

He dashed into the living room, where he found toys and treats—just for him!

"Fuddles, don't touch!"

"Stay away!"

"Be careful!"

But then Fuddles saw
the best gift of all.
A tree!
A tree with
twinkling lights and
glittering stars—
just for him . . .

to climb!

O - O - O - O - O - O!"

Fuddles ran as fast as he could.
Before he knew it, he was . . .

Outside!

He looked around in amazement.

What *was* all this white stuff?

What happened to the green grass and leaves?

Where were all the flowers?

And *brrrrrrrr* . . . . . it was cold!
Very cold.

Fuddles had to get back inside, but now the door was closed.

He called his family, but they didn't hear him or see him.

Maybe the back door was open.

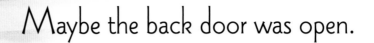

Whoops!

Whoosh!

Bump!

Like a pioneer frontiersman, Fuddles
bravely faced the elements . . .

through the bitter cold
and biting wind . . .

ignoring his icy whiskers, frozen paws, and rumbling tummy.

Where *was* that door?

Danger lurked everywhere.

Plop!

Splat!

Ow!

Who did that?

Fuddles looked up and spotted squirrels! Pesky squirrels.

They had no idea what he was made of, did they?

Fuddles hopped and flopped.
He slid and skidded and slipped.

And somehow, he reached the
top of the tree.

He chased the squirrels to the
end of the branch, and when they
jumped . . .

so did Fuddles.

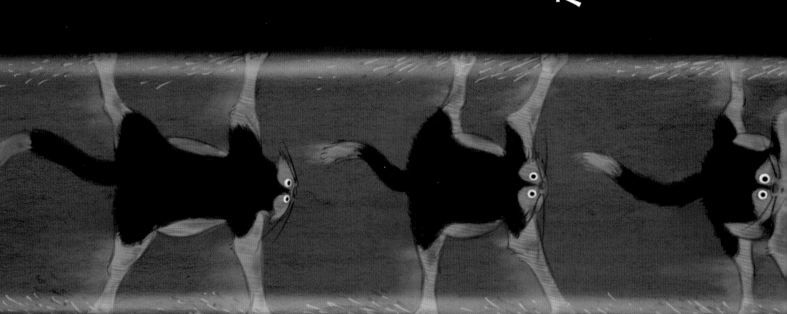

Uh-oh!
It was dark.

And scary.

And dirty.

And smelly.

OOMPH!

"Fuddles! Where have you been?" asked Mom. "Just be glad we didn't light the fireplace yet."

A warm bath . . .

a soft towel . . .

a sweet scent . . .

and a home-cooked meal——

just for him.

Merry Christmas, Fuddles!